KU-727-844

For my wonderful mum who, when she woke up, was not a hippopotamus. T.M.

For Sabine, Lonneke, Jessie and Max. R.C.

Falkirk Council	
BB	
Askews & Holts	
JF JF	£5.99

This paperback edition published in 2012 by Andersen Press Ltd.

Published in Australia by Random House Australia Pty.,

Level 3, 100 Pacific Highway, North Sydney, NSW 2060.

First published in Great Britain in 2011 by Andersen Press Ltd.

Text copyright © Tom MacRae, 2011

Illustration copyright © Ross Collins, 2011

The rights of Tom MacRae and Ross Collins to be identified as

the author and illustrator of this work have been asserted by them in

accordance with the Copyright, Designs and Patents Act, 1988. All rights reserved.

Colour separated in Switzerland by Photolitho AG, Zürich. Printed and bound in Singapore by Tien Wah Press.

Ross Collins has used concentrated watercolour, vinyl colour and pen on watercolour paper in this book.

10   9   8   7   6   5   4   3   2   1

British Library Cataloguing in Publication Data available. ISBN 978 1 84939 359 1

This book has been printed on acid free paper.

WHEN I WOKE UP I WAS A
HIPPOPOTAMUS

Tom MacRae

Ross Collins

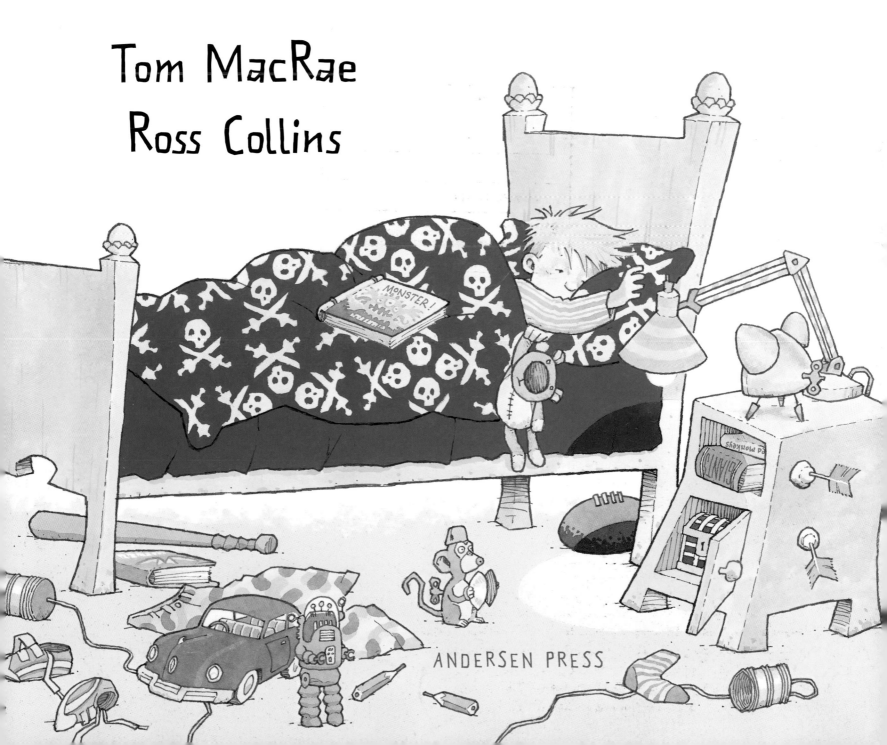

ANDERSEN PRESS

When I woke up I was a

Yawning in the morning, I raised up my sleepy head,
Then took one look out of the window
and got straight back into bed.

"Get up!" said Mum. "Or you'll be late!"

But hippos in their sludge
Don't get up in the morning,
and so I didn't budge.

My tummy wasn't hungry. I wasn't programmed how to eat.
My mouth was made of metal, like my nose and knees and feet.
"Quick, quick!" said Dad. "Come on! Eat up!
We've really got to scoot!"

But robots can't eat
cornflakes. Dad's words
did not compute.

When it was time to go to school I was a . . .

STATUE

I couldn't move a muscle.
I couldn't blink an eye.
I couldn't lift a finger.
I couldn't breathe a sigh.

Mum pushed, then pulled.
Dad pulled, then pushed.
They heaved with all their might.

But my legs were made of granite
and my feet were stuck down tight.

When I got to school I was a . . .
Monkey!

A cheeky little monkey
thought a table was a tree.
I had to climb upon it just to
see what I could see.

I couldn't sit and listen,
and my work was rather slack.
And when the teacher told me off
– I told her off right back!

When it was playtime I was a ...
MONSTER!

A scritchy-scratchy monster with ten scritchy-scratchy claws.
I had fifty scritchy-scratchy teeth in scritchy-scratchy jaws.

The girls all screamed! The boys all ran!
My mouth went munchy-crunch!
Then teacher told me off again
(so I had her for my lunch).

I zoomed up out of orbit,
countdown – 5, 4, 3, 2, 1.
I was nearly reaching light-speed,
poor old Dad he had to run!

My pistons pumped,
my jetpacks jumped
– all full of super fuel.
I had to get to Planet Home
and far from Planet School!

When I was in my bedroom I was a ... GIANT!
My hands were huge as houses, my beard was big and blue.
I was hunting for a human to put in my human stew.
I was crashing round my bedroom – well that's just how giants play.
We're big and loud and noisy. We don't know another way.

But Mum and Dad weren't happy and they yelled out,

"Keep it down!"

But my giant feet were busy as they crushed a tiny town.
"That's it!" cried Mum and Dad.
"You're louder than **TEN** boys!"
And they stomped upstairs to tell me off
for making so much noise.

When Mum and Dad came in they were . . . DRAGONS!

They snarled and growled and stamped and howled and nearly broke the door.
Their wings caught in the curtains and their tails scratched on the floor.

Dad blew a giant smoke ring
with an angry rumbling cough.
Mum wagged a scaly finger –
   then they *really* told me off!

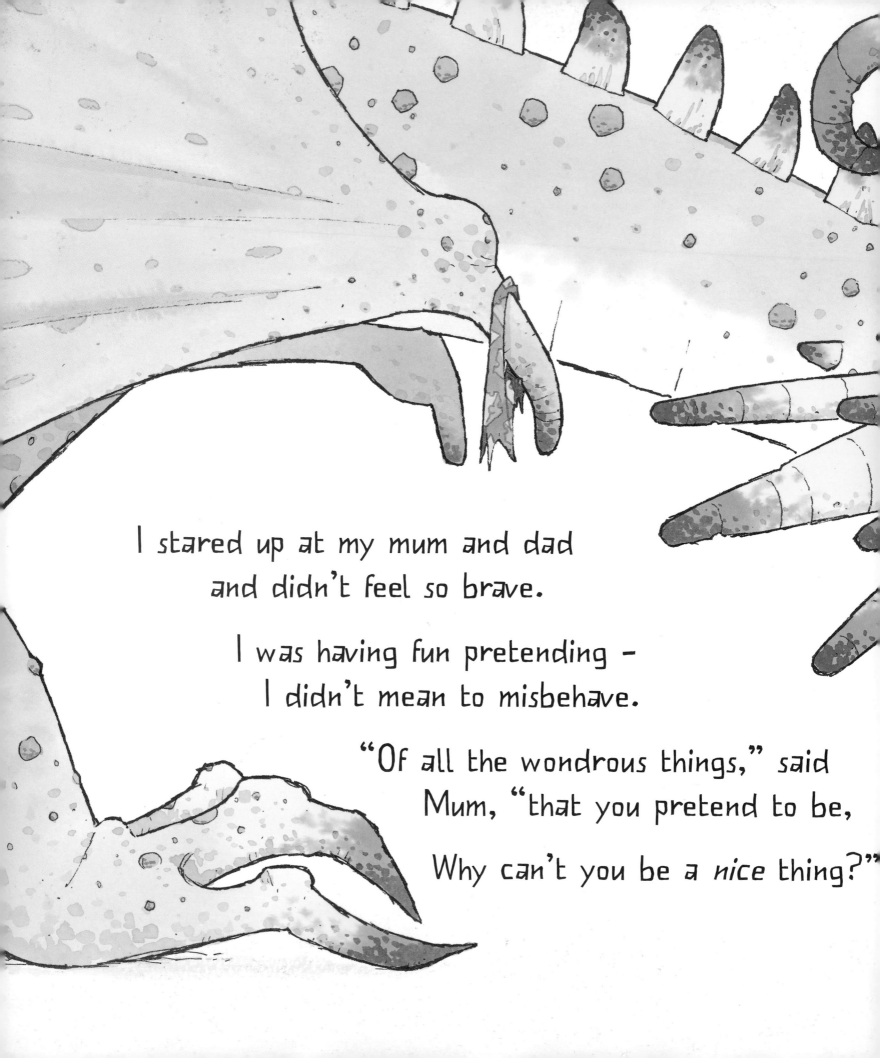

I stared up at my mum and dad
and didn't feel so brave.

I was having fun pretending –
I didn't mean to misbehave.

"Of all the wondrous things," said
Mum, "that you pretend to be,

Why can't you be a *nice* thing?"

So I pretended I was . . .

...ME!

We had a lovely evening.
I helped my dad with tea.

Then I read my mum
a story as I sat
upon her knee.

At bath time we played pirates and we plotted pirate schemes.

Then I snuggled in my duvet . . .

...and dreamed AMAZING DREAMS.

Other books written by Tom MacRae:

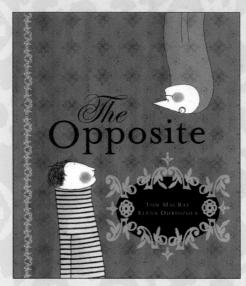

9781842705735

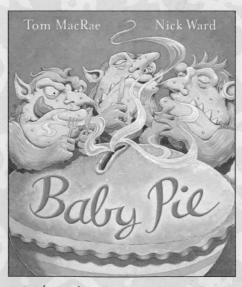

9781842708682